Scared Witless

THIRTEEN EERIE TALES TO TELL

OTHER BOOKS BY
MARTHA HAMILTON AND MITCH WEISS

How & Why Stories
World Tales Kids Can Read & Tell

Noodlehead Stories
World Tales Kids Can Read & Tell

Through the Grapevine
World Tales Kids Can Read & Tell

The Hidden Feast
A Folktale from the American South

Stories in My Pocket
Tales Kids Can Tell

Children Tell Stories
Teaching and Using Storytelling in the Classroom

Scared Witless

THIRTEEN EERIE TALES TO TELL

Martha Hamilton & Mitch Weiss
Illustrated by Kevin Pope

August House Publishers, Inc.
LITTLE ROCK

Published 2006 by August House Publishers, Inc.
P.O. Box 3223, Little Rock, Arkansas 72203
www.augusthouse.com

Printed in the United States of America

Book design by Joy Freeman

10 9 8 7 6 5 4 3 2 1 HB

LIBRARY OF CONGRESS CATALOGING-IN-PUBLICATION DATA

Scared witless : thirteen eerie tales to tell /
Martha Hamilton & Mitch Weiss ; illustrated by Kevin Pope.
p. cm.
Summary: A collection of folktales, primarily from the United States, as well as one
adaptation and two original stories, each followed by tips for novice storytellers.
ISBN-13: 978-0-87483-796-4 (hardcover : alk. paper)
ISBN-10: 0-87483-796-0 (hardcover : alk. paper)
1. Tales. 2. Ghost stories. 3. Horror tales. 4. Storytelling.
[1. Ghosts—Folklore. 2. Horror stories. 3. Folklore. 4. Storytelling—Collections.]
I. Hamilton, Martha. II. Weiss, Mitch, 1951– III. Pope, Kevin, ill.

PZ8.1.S2792 2006
[398.2]—dc22

2006044457

To the youngest "jumpers" in our family—
Bailey, Mollie, and Brian

Acknowledgments

Grateful acknowledgment is made to the following for permission to reprint previously published material: Joseph Bruchac for the story "The Brave Woman and the Flying Head," from *Iroquois Stories* (copyright © 1985 by Joseph Bruchac), adapted for telling by children and used by permission of the author; Betty Lehrman for "The Graveyard Voice," originally published in *The Ghost & I: Scary Stories for Participatory Telling* (copyright © 1985 by Betty Lehrman), adapted for telling by children and used by permission of the author and Yellow Moon Press.

Thanks also to Peter Carroll for permission to adapt and print "The Boy Who Was Afraid of Plants," which was previously unpublished.

Contents

Introduction

Goosebumps, Gasps, and Giggles

Stories are powerful. If a story is well told, listeners feel as if they are in a bit of a trance. Listening to a story can create the same kind of feeling that we get when we sit and stare at a fire. Our bodies relax, and it feels as if we are suspended in time. Storytellers have always loved to tell tales around a campfire because listeners are lulled by the story *and* the fire at the same time. The campfire is the perfect setting to tell a "jump" story, the whole point of which is to startle the listeners. The teller speaks in a slow, spooky voice for much of the story and then surprises listeners with a fast, loud sound such as a scream or a ghost shouting "BOO!"

But you don't have to wait for the perfect setting to tell a scary story. We have been telling stories and teaching others to tell since 1980 and have seen thousands of students tell scary stories effectively in all sorts of settings. If you start by turning the lights down low and telling one of these stories to a friend next time you have a sleepover, you may get hooked. Your newfound confidence may spur you to take the chance and tell for a larger group.

When we teach students of any age to tell, we find that they love to tell many kinds of stories. But their favorites are often either scary stories or funny stories. If they are both scary *and* funny, all the better. Most people, young and old, seem to have a love/hate relationship with being scared. We like to feel a shiver go down our spines as long as we know that what caused it isn't real: it's "just a story" or "just a movie."

So, here's a collection of thirteen eerie tales to give your listeners goosebumps, gasps, and giggles. Some of the stories, such as "The Hairy Toe" and "Unwelcome Company," are our own versions of folktales that have been passed along by word of mouth for generations. Others, such as "The Coffin that Wouldn't Stop," "The Mysterious Rapping Noise," and "The Ghost with Bloody Fingers," are really bad jokes disguised as jump tales. Listeners may groan at the end because these tales fit into the category of "stories so bad they're good." But if your listeners groan, it also means that they realize you've tricked them; they fell for your bad joke! Because listeners never seem to get enough of jump stories, we were inspired to make up some original ones as well.

General Tips for Telling Jump Stories

All of these stories are meant to be told, so we have written them in language that feels comfortable rolling off the tongue. However, since storytelling is an art form, there is not one "right" way to tell a story. There are many ways, and the more different they are, the more interesting the world is. Don't think that you need to memorize exact words to tell a story. Just learn the plot and then tell it in your own words.

To help you get started, we give a few suggestions for telling after each of the thirteen stories. Don't think that our suggestions for movements or expressions are the *only* ideas that will work for telling the story. You may come up with something different that will work just as well, and it will feel more comfortable because it is *your* way.

Here are a few general tips that are important when telling a scary story.

- *Take your time.* If you rush through a scary story, it won't be effective. For the scariest parts, get a little quieter and slow down to "real time" so that listeners feel as if they are in the story. Then there will be a strong contrast when you suddenly say something loud and fast.

- If you want to startle the listeners, it helps to make a quick hand motion at the same time.

- Another effective technique is to look toward one side of the audience just as the ghost or monster is about to say something loud and then jump toward the other side. For example, it works well at the end of "Unwelcome Company" to look with your most scary face toward one side of the audience as you say, "I've come for . . ." Then pause and quickly turn to the other side and point toward them as you say, "YOU!" as loudly as you can. After you say the ending, step back and take a bow so that everyone knows the story is over.

Only "Lost in the Dark" is written as if it really happened to the teller and not someone else. This is called speaking in "first person" and adds to the mystery. This technique would work well with some of the other stories as well. For example, "The Mysterious Rapping Noise" could begin with, "I had finally convinced my parents that I was old enough to stay home alone while they went out to dinner," rather than "Bailey had finally convinced her parents . . ."

For lots of good tips on telling stories, we suggest that you refer to our other books. Some of them include more scary stories. All are available at www.beautyandthebeaststorytellers.com and from the publishers listed below:

- *How & Why Stories: World Tales Kids Can Read & Tell* (August House, 1999) 1-800-284-8784 or www.augusthouse.com. (Recording also available)

- *Noodlehead Stories: World Tales Kids Can Read & Tell* (August House, 2000) 1-800-284-8784 or www.augusthouse.com.

- *Stories in My Pocket: Tales Kids Can Tell* (Fulcrum Publishers, 1996) 1-800-992-2908 or www.fulcrum-resources.com. (Recording also available)

- *The Thing: A Scary Tale with Tips for Telling* (Richard C. Owen Books for Young Learners, forthcoming 2007) 1-800-336-5588 or www.rcowen.com.

- *Through the Grapevine: World Tales Kids Can Read and Tell* (August House, 2001) 1-800-284-8784 or www.augusthouse.com.

- Teachers who would like to teach their students to tell stories will be interested in *Children Tell Stories: Teaching and Using Storytelling in the Classroom*, 2nd edition (Richard C. Owen Publishers, 2005). On the companion DVD to the book, Hannah tells "The Hairy Toe" to her classmates and invited guests at a family storytelling festival. 1-800-336-5588 or www.rcowen.com.

Getting Started

Telling stories involves taking a risk, but it is well worth it. So take these stories, make them your own, and tell them to your friends and family. You may give them goosebumps or even cause a few gasps, but in the end you'll leave them laughing.

Unwelcome Company

A Folktale from the British Isles and the United States

One night, a man settled into his favorite comfy chair in his living room. He took out the book he had been reading, *Frankenstein Meets Godzilla*. The man was happy to finally have some time alone. He couldn't wait to find out how the story was going to end.

But then again, he wasn't sure he wanted to know . . . You see, on the one hand, he *loved* scary stories! But, on the other hand, he *hated* scary stories! Still, he opened the book, and started to read.

Outside, the wind whistled *Shhhhhhh* . . . . . . And off in the distance a wolf howled *Ah-OOOOOOO* . . .

Inside, the man closed the book. "Hmmm! Maybe I'll finish this book . . . tomorrow when it's light out. Tonight, I wish I had some company . . ."

Just then, he heard a *scratch, scratch, scratch* in the chimney.

A creepy voice called, "I'M COMING DOWN . . ."

BAM!

Suddenly two bony skeleton feet tumbled down from the chimney and landed on the floor right by the man's chair.

Outside, the wind whistled *Shhhhhhhh* . . . . . . And off in the distance a wolf howled *Ah-OOOOOOO* . . .

Inside, the man shuddered and shook. This was *not* the kind of company he had wished for.

Before he could jump up, he heard the same *scratch, scratch, scratch* in the chimney.

Again the voice called, "I'M COMING DOWN . . ."

BAM!

At that moment, two long, bony legs tumbled down from the chimney and attached themselves to the feet.

Outside, the wind whistled *Shhhhhhhhh* . . . . . And off in the distance a wolf howled *Ah-OOOOOOO* . . .

Inside, the man sat frozen in fear as he heard the same *scratch, scratch, scratch* in the chimney.

The voice called,
"I'M COMING DOWN . . ."

BAM!

A bony body with two arms tumbled down from the chimney and attached itself to the legs.

Outside, the wind whistled *Shhhhhhhhh* . . . . . And off in the distance a wolf howled *Ah-OOOOOOO* . . .

Inside, the man's heart nearly jumped out of his chest. Once again, he heard the *scratch, scratch, scratch.*

The eerie voice called,
"I'M COMING DOWN . . ."

BAM!

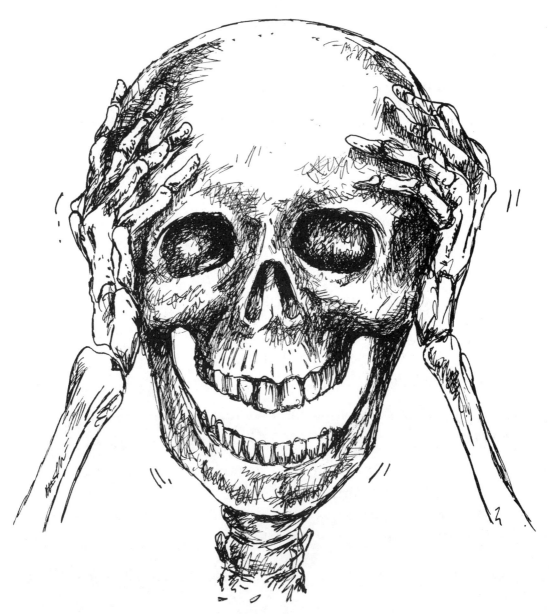

A large, bony head tumbled down from the chimney and attached itself to the rest of the skeleton.

"HA! HA! HA! HA! HA!" cackled the skeleton as it looked right at the man and wiggled its bones about.

At last the man managed to ask, "Wh—what have you come for?"

And the skeleton answered,

"I'VE COME FOR . . .

YOU!"

Tips for telling ————————————————————————————————————— ◗

Listeners love to join in on this story. Here is our suggested introduction:

> I will need your help with some sound effects and
> motions in this story.
> Each time after I say, "Outside, the wind whistled,"
> help me by saying, "Shhhhhhhh . . . . . ."

(Say "Shhhhhhhh . . ." or any spooky whistling sound that feels comfortable for you. Make a slow, swirling motion with your hands at the same time.)

> Try that and do the hand motion with me, too:
> "Shhhhhhhhh . . . ."

(Lead the listeners as you do the whistling sound and hand motion a second time.)

> After I say, "Off in the distance a wolf howled,"
> help me by putting your head back and howling,
> "Ah-OOOOOOO . . ."
> Try that: "Ah-OOOOOOO . . ."

(Again, lead the listeners as you do the sound and motion a second time.)

> You can also join in each time the man in the
> story hears the *"scratch, scratch, scratch."*
> Try that, *very* slowly so it sounds really spooky:
> *"scratch, scratch, scratch."*
> And there's one last sound. It's when the creepy
> voice says,
> "I'M COMING DOWN . . ."

Try that: "I'M COMING DOWN . . ."

Just follow my hand cues and stop making the sounds and doing the motions whenever I stop.

Here's how the story goes . . .

Make all of your instructions and hand signals clear. Say "*scratch, scratch, scratch*" *very* slowly and make hand motions to show scratching. We've found that it helps tellers to slow down if they say "*scratch*" and make the scratching gesture as they look first at one side of the audience, then the middle, and then the other side.

At other times, such as when you say, "*BAM!*" it will surprise the listeners if you say it loudly and quickly, with a little jump toward them to give them a start. Each time a body part falls down, make a hand motion to suggest that something is falling, and pretend to be horrified as you "see" it.

Use a scary voice when the skeleton says, "I'M COMING DOWN . . ." and hold your body and move your hands to make the listeners know it is something like a skeleton or monster speaking. If you feel comfortable doing an evil laugh for the skeleton, that's great. If not, say something like, "The skeleton let out a hideous laugh," and leave it to your listeners' imaginations.

The Coffin that Wouldn't Stop

A Story from the United States

Albert Ward lived all by himself in a big city.

One chilly winter night he was walking down his street toward home. Suddenly, he heard a strange noise behind him.

THUMP! THUMP! THUMP!

Albert's heart began to pound.

THUMP! THUMP! THUMP!

He looked out of the corner of his eye, but he couldn't tell what was making the noise.

Albert walked faster.

The *THUMP! THUMP! THUMP!* grew louder.

At last, he got to his house and turned in at the front walk.

When Albert finally looked back, he saw a *huge* black coffin *THUMP! THUMP! THUMPing!* behind him.

Albert scurried up the porch steps as fast as he could, hoping the coffin would not follow him. But the coffin turned at his house and started *THUMP! THUMP! THUMPing!* toward him!

Albert was shaking so much that he couldn't find the right key. At last, he unlocked the door, rushed inside, and locked it behind him. He gave a big sigh of relief.

"I must have been seeing things," he thought to himself. Then, just to be sure, he *slooowly* pulled up the shade and looked out the window.

YIKES! There was the coffin! It had THUMPed its way onto the porch! With an awful crash, it smashed the door down!

Albert dashed up the stairs to the second floor. But the coffin started up the stairs after him.

THUMP! THUMP! THUMP! Albert's knees jiggled like jello. His eyes bulged like balloons.

"If the coffin makes it up here, it's all over!" he thought.

He grabbed a lamp and threw it at the coffin, hoping to knock it down. But the lamp shattered into a thousand pieces. And the coffin would not stop . . .

THUMP! THUMP! THUMP!

At last, it reached the top of the stairs.

THUMP! THUMP! THUMP!

Closer and closer it came.

THUMP! THUMP! THUMP!

Poor Albert was backed up against the wall.

There was no escaping the horrible coffin!

THUMP!

THUMP!

THUMP!

Luckily, just then Albert remembered something he had in his pocket.

He searched frantically until at last he found it.

Albert took out a cough drop and threw it at the coffin . . .

and the coffin stopped!

Tips for telling

This type of tale is often called a "shaggy dog" story. These are stories that are told as if they are scary or serious, but the ending is a joke; it is usually a silly play on words. In this case the teller plays with the fact that the words "coffin" and "coughing" sound similar.

The *THUMP! THUMP! THUMP!* sound must send a shiver down your listeners' spines, so practice and practice until you feel it is believable. Look in the mirror as you practice; using hand motions and facial expressions at the same time you make the eerie sound will add immensely to the effect.

Be sure that you say "cough drop" clearly. The ending will be a surprise for your listeners, so you want to be sure they understand what you're saying. Then say the ending—"And the coffin stopped!"—with amazement.

Lost in the Dark

A Folktale from the United States

Late one night, I was on my way home when I got lost. As I walked along the dark, dark, road I saw a dark, dark, house. I walked up the dark, dark, path and up the creaky wooden steps. I knocked on the door.

No one answered.

I walked into the dark, dark, house and called out, "Anybody here?"

No one answered.

I walked down a dark, dark, hall and came to a dark, dark, door. I opened the dark, dark, door.

Cr—ee—ee—ee—ak

I walked into the dark, dark room and called out, "Anybody here?"

No one answered.

In the corner of that dark, dark room was a dark, dark chest. I opened the lid of the dark, dark chest.

Cr—ee—ee—ee—ak

Inside the dark, dark chest was . . . a skeleton. Slowly a bony hand rose up out of the dark, dark chest . . .

"GOTCHA!"

Tips for telling

This is a classic "jump" story. Take your time as you tell it, especially each time you repeat "dark, dark." When you open the chest at the end, act this part out. Pretend to slowly open the chest and pause as you "see" the skeleton. Raise one hand slowly upward as you describe the bony hand rising from the chest and then jump forward a bit as you yell, "Gotcha!" For more ideas, see the general tips on telling jump stories in the introduction.

The Boy Who Was Afraid of Plants

Adapted from a Story by Peter Carroll

There were once two brothers named Alan and Peter who loved to tease their younger brother, Andy. One day, when Alan and Peter arrived home from school, they found Andy watching a movie called *Killer Plants from Outer Space*.

The movie started innocently in a beautiful city park. But as night fell, large seedpods began to drop from the sky. By morning the pods had sprouted and were growing quickly.

"Wow! This looks cool," squealed Alan. He and Peter joined Andy in front of the TV.

Soon the plants from outer space were eight feet tall, and their enormous leaves continued to grow. Andy was beginning to look a bit nervous. As they watched, a man entered the park pushing a hot dog cart.

Andy cried, "No! Don't go into the park!"

Just then, a giant plant grabbed the man and devoured him whole. Young Andy was terrified. He ran upstairs, jumped into bed, and hid under the covers.

Alan and Peter doubled over laughing at their little brother. "Help! The big bad plant is going to get me!" they giggled.

That night, during dinner, Andy kept looking suspiciously at the large plant in their dining room. And when it was bedtime, he couldn't get to sleep. Every time he shut his eyes he would see a monster plant smacking its leafy lips.

Meanwhile, his brothers were laughing and plotting. When their mom heard them giggling in the next room, she asked, "What are you boys up to?"

"Oh, nothing," they replied.

Their voices grew quieter as they planned their practical joke.

"Tomorrow, let's cut a few big leaves from the banana tree," said Peter. "Then we can hide in the bushes."

"Great idea!" agreed Alan, with a devilish laugh. "As soon as Andy comes outside, we'll chase him around the yard! He'll scream his little head off!"

The next day after school they couldn't wait to put their plan into action. Alan and Peter quietly made their way to the back porch. Alan took out his official Boy Scout pocketknife and sliced off a few of the big leaves from the banana tree. Then they crept off the porch, hid behind the bush by their back door, and waited for Andy.

Before long, they heard a rustling in a nearby bush.

"What's that?" Peter asked nervously.

The rustling grew louder. The boys tried to see through the jungle of leaves. Suddenly, an enormous, hairy gorilla burst through the bushes. *ROARRRRR!!!*

The gorilla beat its chest and showed its sharp teeth. *ROARRRRR!!!*

Alan and Peter were petrified. They lay behind the bush, unable to move.

But when the gorilla began to plod toward them, they screamed, "Mom! Help! Save us!"

Just then, the gorilla started to chuckle, "Ha! Ha! Ha!" and then broke into a thunderous laugh. "HA! HA! HA!"

Alan and Peter held their breath as the beast raised its arms and removed its head.

"Mom!" they cried in stunned surprise.

Their mom grinned broadly as she wiped the sweat off her forehead. "That's right," she replied. "When I heard you two cooking up that practical joke, I decided I needed to teach you boys a lesson. I knew this old Hallowe'en costume would come in handy one day."

It was a long time before Alan and Peter teased their younger brother again.

Tips for telling

The dialogue in this story makes it really fun to tell. It is important to use your body to show the difference in the characters—young, frightened Andy, the two older brothers as they tease and plot, their suspicious mother, and the gorilla as it roars and laughs.

To practice, try telling the story wordlessly while acting it out in the mirror. See if you think listeners will be able to tell the difference in the characters just by looking at you.

If you don't feel comfortable roaring (or laughing) like the gorilla, say something like, "Suddenly, an enormous, hairy gorilla burst through the bushes and *roared!*" If you use good expression, your listeners will be able to imagine the gorilla's ferocious roar.

The Graveyard Voice

by Betty Lehrman

There was once an ordinary man named John, who was married to a beautiful woman named Mary, who was also—*very* ordinary. And they had two lovely children named Jimmy and Jeanie who were also—*very* ordinary.

There was one extraordinary thing about this family—they lived right next door to the . . . graveyard.

And every day John walked to and from work through the . . . graveyard.

Now, he could have walked around it, but that would have taken twenty minutes longer, and John was a very busy man. So day after day, week after week, and month after month, he walked to and from work through the . . . graveyard.

This story takes place in late October, just a couple of days before Hallowe'en. The clocks had just been turned back the weekend before. So when John got ready to leave his office at his usual time . . . 5:30 . . . for his walk home through the . . . graveyard . . . it was already dark outside.

As he approached the graveyard gate he could hear the wind blowing through the trees . . . WOOOOOO . . . and the leaves skittering across the ground . . . *ch ch ch ch ch ch* . . . And then suddenly, he heard a strange voice from the graveyard calling out,

"TURN ME OVER . . . TURN ME OVER."

John scurried home as fast as he could!

When he got there—*phew!*—he told his wife, Mary, and his children, Jimmy and Jeanie, what he had heard in the graveyard.

But his wife said, "Dear!"

And his children said, "Daddy! There's nothing in the graveyard!"

The next day was the day before Hallowe'en. John got ready to leave the office at his usual time . . . 5:30 . . . for his walk home through the . . . graveyard.

As he approached the graveyard gate, he could hear the wind blowing through the trees . . . *WOOOOOO* . . . and the leaves skittering across the ground . . . *ch ch ch ch ch ch* . . . And once again, he heard a strange voice moaning,

"TURN ME OVER . . . TURN ME OVER."

John scurried home as fast as he could!

When he got there—*phew!*—he told his wife, Mary, and his children, Jimmy and Jeanie, what he had heard in the graveyard.

But his wife said, "Dear!"

And his children said, "Daddy! There's nothing in the graveyard!"

The next night it was . . . Hallowe'en.

Despite what his beautiful wife, Mary, and his lovely children, Jimmy and Jeanie, said, John knew there was something in the graveyard.

And he was determined to find out what it was.

John got ready to leave the office at his usual time . . . 5:30 . . . for his walk home through the . . . graveyard.

As he approached the graveyard gate, a huge cloud passed over the moon. It was pitch black.

In the darkness, he could hear the wind blowing through the trees . . . WOOOOOO . . . and the leaves skittering across the ground . . . *ch ch ch ch ch ch* . . . Again, the same strange voice pleaded,

"TURN ME OVER . . . TURN ME OVER."

This time John did not go running home. He followed the voice through the graveyard gate, around some trees, and by some shrubs. At last, he found himself right in the middle of the . . . graveyard.

And there, in front of him, was a huge marble crypt surrounded by a fence. John said to himself, "That must be where the voice is coming from."

So he opened up the gate . . . *Creeeeeaaaaaaak!*

He began to walk down the steps toward the door. As he walked, he counted—there were *thirteen* steps.

When he reached the door, he put his ear to it. And sure enough, he heard the voice from behind the door . . .

"TURN ME OVER . . . TURN ME OVER."

John put his hand on the doorknob and opened it . . . *Creeeeeaaaaaaak!*

He stepped inside, and there, on the floor, was a huge pile of red hot flaming coals!

And on top of the coals was a metal grill!

And on top of the grill was an enormous . . .

. . . hamburger!?!

It was done only on one side. And the poor hamburger was begging,

"TURN ME OVER . . . TURN ME OVER."

So John walked up to the grill.

There happened to be a huge spatula sitting beside it. He picked up the spatula, put it under the hamburger, and *turned* it over.

And the hamburger politely said,

"THANK YOU. THANK YOU."

And that's the story of "The Graveyard Voice."

Thank *you* for listening.

Tips for telling

This is a fun participatory story. You are the leader, so it's important that you model for your listeners by using excellent expression. To get them to join in with you as you tell this story, we recommend that you introduce it with something like the following:

I'm going to need your help telling this story.

I'll teach you a few sound effects and motions that will help create a spooky setting.

The first sound we need is wind blowing through the trees.

It sounds like this:

WOOOOOO . . .

(As you say this, make a slow, spooky motion with your hands to show swirling wind.)

Now you try it—do the motion, too:

WOOOOOO . . .

(Lead the listeners as you make the sounds and motions a second time.)

Then we need the sound of dry, crunchy leaves skittering across the ground in late fall.

It sounds like this . . .

ch ch ch ch ch ch . . .

(Make a motion with your hands and fingers that will help listeners picture this.)

Try it . . .

ch ch ch ch ch ch . . .

Next is a scary, pleading voice that says, "Turn me over . . . Turn me over," the first time with a low pitch, and the second with a higher pitch.

Try it:

"TURN ME OVER . . . TURN ME OVER."

(You want the listeners to picture some kind of scary creature such as a mummy saying this. One thing that works well is to hold both arms out in front of you as if you are a zombie, and move your arms slowly from one side to the other as you plead, "Turn me over . . . Turn me over.")

The last sound effect is a creaky door opening
Let's all do it together:

Creeeeeaaaaaaaak!

So please join in when those sounds come up.
Ready or not, here's how the story goes . . .

Pause just before you say "graveyard" with a slow, spooky tone the first time. Afterward, if you pause just before you say it the second time and motion toward your listeners, they will join in and say it with you. Since you say "graveyard" many times throughout the story, it will be too much if you do this every time. Choose a few perfect spots and give the listeners their cue, which is the pause just beforehand.

When you say "Dear" and "Daddy," put your best "Have you gone crazy?" expression in your body and on your face. Try to show a difference between John's wife and his kids by holding your body in a different position for each.

The Hairy Toe

A Folktale from the United States

One evening, an old woman was pulling up weeds in her garden when she found a big, hairy toe.

"Mmm!" she said to herself. "This will taste delicious in my soup."

She picked it up, brought it into the house, and put it into her refrigerator.

Late that night, after the old woman climbed the stairs and got into bed, she thought she heard something way down the road cry, "WHERE'S MY HAIRY TOE? WHO'S GOT MY HAIRY TOE?"

"What was that?" she wondered. She listened carefully, but when she didn't hear it again, she soon fell fast asleep.

A little while later, she was awakened by something in her garden moaning, "WHERE'S MY HAIRY TOE? WHO'S GOT MY HAIRY TOE?"

"That must have been a dream," she thought. But before she could fall asleep again, she heard the voice right by her front door. "WHERE'S MY HAIRY TOE? WHO'S GOT MY HAIRY TOE?"

Then the front door opened, *Cr—ee—ee—ak . . .*

Now the woman knew she wasn't dreaming. She was terrified!

From the bottom of the stairs she heard the voice wail, "WHERE'S MY HAIRY TOE? WHO'S GOT MY HAIRY TOE?"

Shivering and shaking, the old woman pulled the covers over her head.

By now, the voice was at her bedroom door. "WHERE'S MY HAIRY TOE? WHO'S GOT MY HAIRY TOE?"

The old woman lay there, shaking under her blankets. The bedroom door opened with a loud *Cr—ee—ee—ak* . . . and something began to move toward her, calling out, "WHERE'S MY HAIRY TOE? WHO'S GOT MY HAIRY TOE?"

The old woman could hear the thing walk right up to her bed. "WHERE'S MY HAIRY TOE? WHO'S GOT MY HAIRY TOE?

"YOU'VE GOT IT!"

Tips for telling

This is another classic jump story. At the beginning, pretend to pick up a big, ugly, hairy toe and look at it with an appropriate expression. When the woman hears the voice down the road, make your listeners feel as if they are part of the story by looking them right in the eyes each time you say, "WHERE'S MY HAIRY TOE? WHO'S GOT MY HAIRY TOE?" Move a bit closer to them each time the voice gets closer. For more ideas, see the general tips on telling jump stories in the introduction.

The Terrifying Trick

An Original Story

There was a boy who was born on April Fool's Day. On his birthday, he always played a trick on his mom.

Once, he hid his toy snake under her pillow. Another time, he put food coloring in the milk to make it turn red. Still another time, he put sugar in the salt shaker.

Luckily, his mom was a good sport. She loved his tricks because they always made her laugh. And since it was his birthday, she couldn't get mad at him.

One April Fool's Day, the boy decided to give his mom a good fright. He stood in the hallway just outside the door to her room.

He waited patiently.

When she opened the door, he jumped out, held his arms up, and yelled, "BOO!"

His mom was so startled that she screamed, "Ahhhhhhh!!!"

This took the boy by surprise and he screamed loudest of all, "AHHHHHHHHHHHH!"

Although he had scared his mother, her reaction had scared *him* even more!

They both started to laugh.

"I guess your trick worked a little *too* well this time," giggled Mom.

"Yes, I guess it did," agreed the boy.

After that, the boy didn't stop playing tricks on his mother. But he stuck to funny ones rather than scary ones.

Tips for telling

This is an original story that was inspired by something that happened to us. One day Martha decided to scare Mitch and, just like the boy in the story, was so startled by his reaction that she screamed louder than him! When you tell this story, try to vary your body positions during the part where the boy scares his mom. Here's one sequence that works: Lunge with both hands forward when the boys says, "BOO!" Then jump backward when his mother screams. Keep in mind that her reaction is so loud that it causes him to jump and scream. To show the boy's reaction, change to a different position such as putting your hands to your head or on your heart. Because this is the most dramatic part of the story, practice it a lot until you feel that it is truly convincing.

The Ghost with Bloody Fingers

A Folktale from the United States

A woman sat in a comfy chair in her living room, reading a good book. From off in the distance, she heard a voice wailing, "I AM THE GHOST WITH BLOODY FINGERS RISING FROM MY GRAVE."

The woman was so frightened that her hair stood out like porcupine quills. A little while later she heard, "I AM THE GHOST WITH BLOODY FINGERS COMING DOWN THE ROAD."

The woman's eyes got so big that her eyebrows almost reached the top of her head. Then the voice was louder: "I AM THE GHOST WITH BLOODY FINGERS OPENING YOUR GATE." —*Cr—ee—ee—ee—ak—*

An eerie shiver went down the woman's spine.

"I AM THE GHOST WITH BLOODY FINGERS WALKING UP YOUR PATH."

She felt a terrifying tingle all the way down to her toes.

"I am the GHOST WITH BLOODY FINGERS KNOCKING AT YOUR DOOR."*BAM! BAM! BAM!*

The woman's heart went, *Ba-Boom! Ba-Boom! Ba-Boom!*

"I AM THE GHOST WITH BLOODY FINGERS FLOATING THROUGH YOUR DOOR."

An icy chill filled the room as the ghost drifted over toward her and cried, "I AM THE GHOST WITH BLOODY FINGERS LOOKING YOU IN THE EYE."

Frozen with fear, the woman managed to ask, "Wh-what do you w-want?"

The grisly ghost held up his bloody fingers and groaned,

"I WANT . . . a few Band-aids, please?"

Tips for telling

This is another "shaggy dog" story. (See the tips for "The Coffin that Wouldn't Stop.") Use a spooky voice for the ghost; you may want to make a ghostly, floating motion with your arms at the same time. It is also effective to hold both hands in front of you and wiggle your fingers. Be sure to hold your fingers high enough so that listeners will be able to see them.

As the ghost gets closer, move up toward the listeners. When you get to the last sentence, say "I WANT" with the same spooky ghost voice. That will make the listeners think something awful is going to happen. Then pause and change your tone to whiny when you say, "A few Band-aids, please?"

The Red Satin Ribbon

A Folktale from Europe and the United States

Sam and Sue lived next door to each other from the time they were born. Every day they played together. Sam *loved* Sue and Sue *loved* Sam.

Sam thought Sue was the sweetest, smartest, and most gorgeous girl he'd ever met. She wore such bright, colorful clothes, and every day she wore a red satin ribbon around her neck.

Sue thought that Sam was the nicest, most considerate, and most handsome boy in the world. Sam *loved* Sue and Sue *loved* Sam.

They went to kindergarten and then first grade together, and every day Sue wore that red ribbon around her neck. Sam began to wonder why Sue always wore that ribbon.

One day, he just had to ask, "Susie, why do you always wear that red ribbon around your neck?"

"Oh, I'll tell you later, Sammy," said Sue shyly.

The years passed by, and still Sam *loved* Sue and Sue *loved* Sam. They went steady all through high school, and every day Sue wore that ribbon around her neck. Sam continued to ask her about it but she'd just say, "I'll tell you later!"

It was the only secret that Sue kept from Sam, but still Sam *loved* Sue and Sue *loved* Sam.

At last, it was the night of the senior prom. Naturally, Sue and Sam went together. Sue wore a beautiful red satin gown to match the ribbon around her neck.

"Sue, why do you always wear that red ribbon?" Sam begged.

"Why do you always ask me that?" snapped Sue. "It's none of your business! If I feel like it, maybe I'll tell you later."

The years passed by, and, although they argued now and then, still Sam *loved* Sue and Sue *loved* Sam. Eventually, they became engaged.

On their wedding day, Sam pleaded, "Sue, why do you always wear that red ribbon around your neck? Can't you take it off just this once?"

"Sammy, darling," said Sue, firmly yet lovingly, "I'll take this ribbon off when I'm good and ready. Now please, let's not argue on our wedding day."

The years passed by, and still Sam *loved* Sue and Sue *loved* Sam. They had two children and several grandchildren. Every day Sue wore that red satin ribbon around her neck. Sam continued to ask her about it, but each time she'd say, "I'll tell you later!"

At last, it was their fiftieth wedding anniversary. Sam was sure that Sue would finally tell him her secret after their many years together.

"Sue, won't you tell me your secret?" said Sam. "Why do you always wear that red satin ribbon around your neck?"

"Sammy, don't you ever get tired of asking me that?" replied Sue. "If I've told you once, I've told you a thousand times. I'll tell you later!"

The years passed by, and still Sam *loved* Sue and Sue *loved* Sam. But then Sue grew ill, and finally she was on her deathbed. Sam knew they had had a wonderful life together, but still he was heartbroken. And there was one thing he had to know before she died.

Kneeling by her bed, tears streaming down his cheeks, he pleaded with her one last time, "Susie, we've known each other for more than eighty years, and every day you've worn that red ribbon tied around your neck. Won't you please tell me why you wear it?"

"Well, Sam, you've been so patient all these years," said Sue, her voice shaking. "If you must know, I'll show you."

With her last bit of strength, Sue took hold of one end of the red satin ribbon and began to untie it,

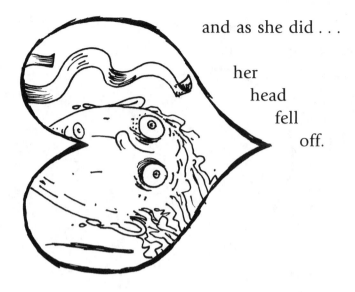

and as she did . . .

her
head
fell
off.

Tips for telling

We have told this story for twenty-five years and still enjoy it, especially the surprise ending. This tale is unusual in that it can be told for Valentine's Day *and* Hallowe'en! If you enjoy doing character voices, do little-kid voices for young Sam and Sue, older voices for them when it's their fiftieth wedding anniversary, and somewhat shaky voices when Sue is on her deathbed. Use body language and expression in your voice to show that, as time passes, Sam gets more and more curious about why Sue wears the ribbon. At the same time, show that Sue grows more frustrated with his frequent questions.

As you say the last sentence, it's important to go very slowly to keep listeners in suspense about why Sue has always worn the red ribbon. When you say "her head fell off," use lots of expression—amazement or confusion or disgust, or perhaps a combination of all these feelings. Before we begin the story, we tell listeners that if they know the ending, they can join in and say the last four words with us, but that they shouldn't tell anyone *before* that.

The Strange White Thing in the Road

A Folktale from the Southern United States

Late one foggy night, a man was walking along a dusty road on his way home. He passed some houses, some fields, the church, and . . . the graveyard.

Now, walking near a graveyard at dark might scare you or me, but not that man. He had no fear.

As he passed the graveyard, he saw something white in the road up ahead. It was about the size of a possum.

"Hmmm. I wonder what that could be," he thought.

Now, you or I might have tucked tail and run, but not that man. He walked up to the white thing and gave it a kick to get it out of his way, the way one might kick a stone.

Suddenly, the white thing swelled up as big as a dog!

Now, you or I might have screamed, or fainted, or fallen down dead from fright. But not that man. He was determined to get that thing out of his way, so he gave it another kick.

This time the white thing swelled up as big as a horse! It floated around the man and glared at him with its evil eyes.

"BOO!" it shouted.

Now that man knew what the white thing was—A GHOST!

And he did exactly what you or I would have done—he tore off down the road! In fact, he ran *so* fast that his feet almost made it home before the rest of his body.

After that, whenever he walked home at night, he always took the long way around town so he wouldn't have to pass the graveyard. And he warned the villagers, "Whatever you do, don't ever kick a ghost!"

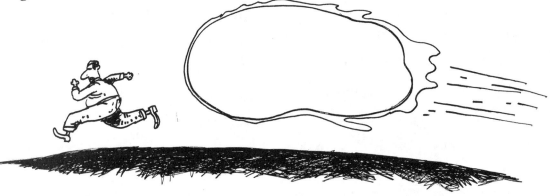

Tips for telling

At the beginning, as you describe the man walking home, it will help listeners picture the man's village if you point toward where the houses, fields, and church would be. Then set the mood for the rest of the story as you say "graveyard" in a slow, spooky tone. Each time the white thing swells up in front of the man, pretend to see it with your eyes in order to help your listeners picture it. When the man warns the other villagers at the very end, look around at your listeners so that they will feel as if they are part of the story. Point your finger in warning as you say the last line *very* slowly.

The Brave Woman and the Flying Head

A Story of the Iroquois Indians

Once a woman was walking to a nearby village with her baby on her back. She was taking food to her relatives because their crops had not done well that year.

When she was deep in the forest, she heard a terrible sound. It was the sound of trees being knocked down, the sound of a great wind rushing in her direction.

She looked back, and there, far above the treetops, was a Flying Head.

Flying Heads are awful creatures. They have huge heads with long, trailing hair—and no bodies. Instead, they have two great paws like those of a bear attached to their heads. And Flying Heads are always hungry.

They fly about the earth searching for food. When they find some, they grab it with their paws and shove it into their gigantic mouths.

The woman knew that the Flying Head would soon catch her human scent, so she would have to think of a way to distract it. She quickly took the food from her pack, scattered it in every direction, and began to run.

Soon, just as the woman had feared, the Flying Head caught her scent. It flew through the forest, following her trail. When it came to the scattered food, it began to eat and did not stop until every bite

49

was gone. By this time, the woman was far ahead on the path. But the Flying Head was as swift as the wind and soon caught up to her.

As the woman looked back, she saw the Flying Head close behind her, reaching out its enormous paws to grab her.

This woman had once heard a wise elder say that the moccasin of a tiny child holds great power for good. So, quick as a wink, she tossed one of her son's small shoes behind her into the monster's path.

The Flying Head grabbed at the moccasin but missed. Its long hair got tangled in the brush beside the path. Growling, it rolled into a patch of brambles where its long hair was caught.

Meanwhile, the woman ran as swiftly as a fox until she was so out of breath that she couldn't run any more. So she climbed high into a tall white pine tree. She whispered to her baby, "Be still. The monster will never find us up here."

It was not long before the Flying Head untangled itself from the brambles. With a terrible roar, it flew through the air, following the woman's trail. Soon it came to the foot of the tree and sniffed about, shouting, "Where has she gone? Why can't I smell her any longer?"

Just then, the woman's baby reached out and knocked loose a tiny branch. It fell down, down, and hit the Flying Head.

The monster let out a roar. In anger it struck the tree with such a blow that it knocked loose a huge dead limb. The limb fell right on top of the Flying Head and pinned it to the ground.

While the monster struggled to get free, the woman climbed down from the pine tree and dashed off. She ran and ran until at last she reached her lodge. She burst inside and made a fire to warm herself and the baby.

At last, she felt safe. But when the baby started to cry, she realized he must be hungry. She looked around for something to eat, but all that was left were a few chestnuts. She took a handful and threw them onto the fire to cook.

Meanwhile, the terrible Flying Head finally managed to get out from under the tree limb. Filled with rage, it followed the trail of the woman right to her lodge. It flew up and looked down through the smoke hole, ready to swoop in and grab her.

But just then, the Flying Head saw the woman reach into the fire. She took out something that looked like a burning coal and thrust it into her mouth.

"OHHH!" growled the monster. "She is eating fire! I didn't know that fire is good to eat!"

It dove down through the smoke hole, grabbed all the coals, and shoved them deep into its mouth.

As the fire started to burn inside it, the Flying Head let out a scream that was heard for miles. Then it flew out the smoke hole . . . and was gone.

From that day on, the village of the woman who was brave and did not lose her courage was never again bothered by the Flying Head.

Tips for telling

When the woman first sees the Flying Head, have an expression of horror and dread as you look above the heads of your listeners and pretend to see it. This will help listeners to create their own images of the creature in their minds. Put lots of expression on your face and in your voice to convey the Flying Head's rage throughout the story and its excitement at the end when it thinks that fire is good to eat.

The Iroquois Indians do not tell traditional tales such as this one during the summer. Stories are thought to be so powerful that even plants will stop to listen and not grow. They tell them only between the first frost in the fall and the last frost in the spring. It is important to respect such traditions if you choose to tell a story that comes from a culture that is not your own. So don't tell this story in the summer!

The Mysterious Rapping Noise

Inspired by a Folktale from the Midwestern United States

Bailey had finally convinced her parents that she was old enough to stay home alone while they went out to dinner.

"Don't open the door if someone knocks," warned her dad.

"Just call us if you need us," said mom.

"I'll be fine. I can take care of myself," Bailey assured them.

At last, her mom and dad left, still looking a bit nervous. But Bailey was calm and collected.

She went upstairs, settled into a chair in her bedroom, and picked up the book she was reading—*The Return of the Vicious Vampire.*

Just as the coffin lid creaked open and the vampire climbed out, Bailey heard a strange sound.

RAP! RAP! RAP!

"What's that?" she thought. She sat perfectly still and listened, but didn't hear anything.

But as soon as she went back to reading, she heard the noise again. This time it was louder.

RAP! RAP! RAP!

"Is my mind playing tricks?" she wondered.

But there it was again.

RAP! RAP! RAP!

Now she knew it was real.

What was that noise? And where was it coming from?

Bailey thought about calling her parents but was afraid they would never let her stay at home alone again.

RAP! RAP! RAP!

Bailey knew that she had to investigate. She cautiously opened her bedroom door and looked both ways.

RAP! RAP! RAP!

The noise seemed to be coming from the first floor. She held tightly to the banister as she crept down the stairs.

RAP! RAP! RAP!

She followed the noise to a closet in the hall.

RAP! RAP! RAP!

As Bailey stood in front of the closet, the pounding of her heart was almost as loud as the *RAP! RAP! RAP!*

It took every bit of her courage to put her hand on the doorknob. She slowly turned it, expecting the worst.

RAP! RAP! RAP!

When she finally opened the door she saw what was making the horrible rapping noise.

It was . . .

a roll of wrapping paper.

Tips for telling

This is our modern version of an old story. It is yet another "shaggy dog" story. (See the tips for "The Coffin that Wouldn't Stop" and "The Ghost with Bloody Fingers.") In this case, the teller tricks the listener because the words "rapping" and "wrapping" sound the same even though they have different meanings.

Create a mood as if this were a real ghost story. Try different ways of saying, *"RAP! RAP! RAP!"* (a raspy, deep pitch works well) until you find a way that sounds creepy and spooky enough. Adding hand motions as you say each *"RAP!"* also adds to the effect. Look at yourself in the mirror to make sure that your facial expression matches the spooky feeling in your voice. Don't let on that it isn't serious until you say "a roll of wrapping paper" at the very end.

The Girl Who Scared Herself

An Original Story

There was a girl who loved to draw.

She also liked scary things.

One afternoon, she sat on her bed and leaned back against a pillow. She drew a dark, haunted house and a full moon in the sky.

"This isn't scary enough," she thought. "It needs a creepy cloud that looks like a hideous monster."

After she drew that, she thought, "That's good, but it still needs more." So she added a huge old tree with long, dangling branches. They looked like hands that would grab anyone who walked by.

"Hmm. It's still not scary enough," she thought.

So she drew a black cat with glowing eyes. It sat on the front porch saying, "*Pssssssssst . . . . .*"

After she drew the cat, she stopped and looked at the drawing. She thought it might need one more scary thing.

But she was too tired to draw any more.

She closed her eyes to take a nap.

Soon she started to dream.

In the dream she saw a dark, haunted house and a full moon in the sky. There was a creepy cloud that looked like a hideous monster.

Beside the house was a huge old tree with long, dangling branches. They looked like hands that would grab anyone who walked by.

On the front porch was a black cat with glowing eyes saying, "*Pssssssssst . . .*"

And hiding behind a bush there was . . . A GHOST!

"Ahhhhhhhhhhhhhh!" she screamed.

This woke her up. She sat bolt upright in the bed.

The girl looked at the drawing in front of her. When she saw there was no ghost in the drawing, a little shiver went down her spine.

"I have to admit that the ghost adds a nice touch," she thought. So she drew the ghost into the drawing.

"Now it's the *perfect* scary picture."

Feeling satisfied, she went to the kitchen, put her drawing on the refrigerator, and ran outside to play.

Tips for telling

As the girl draws the picture, pretend to draw each thing and then look at the drawing to see if it's scary enough. When you describe the tree with long, dangling branches, you may want to move up toward your listeners and dangle your arms with a slow, spooky, ghostlike motion. Pretend to be an evil, sneaky cat as you say *"Pssssssssst . . ."* To practice, look in the mirror to find what makes you look wicked; raising your eyebrows up and down can be quite effective.

Story Sources

The motifs referred to in the source notes that follow are from *The Storyteller's Sourcebook: A Subject, Title, and Motif Index to Folklore Collections for Children* by Margaret Read MacDonald (Detroit: Gale, 1982) and the second edition by MacDonald and Brian W. Sturm (Detroit: Gale, 2001).

The Boy Who Was Afraid of Plants

This story was adapted with the permission of our good friend, filmmaker Peter Carroll. Peter filmed a short documentary of our work that is included as a companion DVD to our book, *Children Tell Stories: Teaching and Using Storytelling in the Classroom* (Katonah, New York: Richard C. Owen Publishers, 2005). One of the things that he filmed was a class of third graders learning and telling stories. Peter was so impressed by their courage and willingness to take the risks involved with telling a story that he wrote and told this family story to them. The students enjoyed it so much that we asked Peter's permission to shorten it for telling by children. Peter says that the part about how he and Alan teased young Andy about being terrified by a movie about killer plants is really true. As for the gorilla part, well . . .

The Brave Woman and the Flying Head

This story was adapted with the permission of storyteller Joseph Bruchac from *Iroquois Stories: Heroes and Heroines, Monsters and Magic* (Trumansburg, New York: Crossing Press, 1985).

The Coffin that Wouldn't Stop

The major motif of this story is Z13.4.1 *Man is chased by coffin.* Versions are found in *One Potato, Two Potato: The Secret Education of American Children* by Mary and Herbert Knapp (New York: W.W. Norton, 1976), pp. 247–248; and in "Tall Tales and 'Sells' from Indiana University Students," by Ernest W. Baughman and Clayton A. Holaday, *Hoosier Folklore Bulletin*, 3:4, December 1944, p. 68.

The Ghost with Bloody Fingers

We first heard this story told by a four-year-old named Morgan Hardy almost twenty years ago. The main motif is Z.13.4.1.1 *Chased by "Ghost* of the Bloody Fingers." Versions can be found in *Scary Stories to Tell in the Dark* by Alvin Schwartz (New York: Harper Trophy, 1981); and in *Strange and Spooky Stories* by Andrew Fusek Peters (Brookfield, Connecticut: Millbrook Press, 1997).

The Girl Who Scared Herself

We made this one up.

The Graveyard Voice

This story was adapted with the permission of storyteller Betty Lehrman who first published a version in *The Ghost & I: Scary Stories for Participatory Telling*, edited by Jennifer Justice (Cambridge, Massachusetts: Yellow Moon Press, 1992). When we asked Betty if she knew of other versions of the tale, she wrote, "I have looked for other versions, but never found one. I really don't think I made it up—I first remember telling it to a group of kids one night at a summer camp in the early '80s. At that point I felt like I was remembering it, although I have no idea from where. The only time I heard of someone else telling it was at a Hallowe'en festival in Boston when my listeners told me that a librarian in the next room had told the same story. When I asked her where she found it, she said she heard a storyteller tell it at a library in Halifax, Massachusetts, many years before. I had once had a gig in the library in Halifax—so she got it from me!"

The Hairy Toe

The main motif of this folktale is E235 *Return from dead to punish theft of part of corpse.* Similar stories can be found in *Scary Stories to Tell in the Dark* by Alvin Schwartz (New York: Harper Trophy, 1981); *Diane Goode's Book of Scary Stories and Songs* (New York: Dutton, 1994); *The Book of Negro Folklore* edited by Langston Hughes and Arna Bontemps (New York: Dodd, Mead & Co., 1958); and *Grandfather Tales* by Richard Chase (Boston: Houghton Mifflin, 1948).

Lost in the Dark

The major motif of this story is Z13.1.4 *Person enters dark, dark house . . . Ghost jumps out.* Our version of this traditional tale from the United States was inspired by "The Dark, Dark House" in *The Parent's Guide to Storytelling* by Margaret Read MacDonald (Little Rock: August House, 2001); and "Dark, Dark, Dark" in *The Thing at the Foot of the Bed and Other Scary Tales* by Maria Leach (Cleveland: World, 1959).

The Mysterious Rapping Noise

This is our modern version of an old story. Other versions can be found in *Witches, Wit, and a Werewolf* by Jeanne B. Hardendorff (Philadelphia: J.B. Lippincott, 1971); *Tomfoolery: Trickery and Foolery with Words* by Alvin Schwartz (Philadelphia: J.B. Lippincott, 1973); and "Tall Tales and 'Sells' from Indiana University Students," by Ernest W. Baughman and Clayton A. Holaday, *Hoosier Folklore Bulletin* 3: 4, December 1944, pp. 68–69.

The Red Satin Ribbon

The major motif of this story is Z13.4.4.1 *The yellow ribbon*. We found versions in *The Rainbow Book of American Folktales and Legends* by Maria Leach (Cleveland: World, 1958); and in *In a Dark, Dark Room and Other Scary Stories* by Alvin Schwartz (New York: HarperTrophy, 1985). Folklorist Leach noted that this folktale is the offspring of an old European folk motif where a person has a strange red thread around his neck that turns out to be the mark that was caused when he was decapitated. Washington Irving's "The Adventure of the German Student" in his *Tales of a Traveler* included this motif.

The Strange White Thing in the Road

The major motif of this story is E599.15 *Don't Ever Kick a Ghost*. A version appears in *The Thing at the Foot of the Bed and Other Scary Tales* by Maria Leach (Cleveland: World, 1959); Leach's source was the *Frank C. Brown Collection of North Carolina Folklore*, Volume 1 (Durham, North Carolina: Duke University Press, 1952).

The Terrifying Trick

This is an original story based on something that happened to us.

Unwelcome Company

This story is really our own but it was inspired by the motif *Z13.1.1 The Strange Visitor*, where a body assembles itself piece by piece. Because we had seen many child tellers have success with "The Graveyard Voice," we wanted to create another audience participation story that would be simple enough for children to be able to teach listeners to join in.